Disney

First edition

Published by Ladybird Books Ltd Loughborough Leicestershire UK

Printed in England (3)

WINNIE THE POOH
and the honey tree

Ladybird Books

Christopher Robin and Pooh

Once there was a boy
named Christopher Robin
who lived with his friends in
an enchanted place called the
Hundred Acre Wood.

Christopher Robin had lots of friends.
There was Piglet, Kanga and Baby Roo,

Owl, Eeyore, Tigger and Rabbit. But his very best friend was Winnie the Pooh, sometimes called Pooh for short.

Winnie the Pooh and Christopher Robin had many exciting adventures together. And they all happened in the Hundred Acre Wood, right in the middle of the Forest.

Winnie the Pooh lived in a cosy house in the Forest, under the name of Sanders. That meant there was a sign over his door that said "Sanders", and Pooh lived under it.

Early one morning, Pooh was sitting on a log just outside his door. He often sat there when he had Important Things to think about.

This morning, Pooh was thinking about his favourite thing in all the world – honey. He loved honey more than anything else, and he ate it for breakfast, lunch, tea and supper – not to mention elevenses and when he wanted A Little Something in between.

Pooh was thinking dreamily about all his lovely honey pots, when he heard his clock chime. That meant it was time to do something – but what? Pooh couldn't remember.

Pooh thought and thought. He closed his eyes and concentrated as hard as he could. He tapped his forehead. "Think, think, think," he told himself.

It wasn't until he heard his clock chime again that Pooh finally did remember. "Oh, yes," he said. "It's time for my Stoutness Exercises!"

So in he went.

Pooh's Stoutness Exercises

Because Pooh ate so much honey, he was inclined to be a bit fat. So he made certain to do his Stoutness Exercises faithfully each morning. After all, he didn't want to get so fat that he burst at the seams!

Pooh stood in front of the mirror, ready to begin. He enjoyed his exercises, and he had made up a little song to go with them:

"When I up, down, touch the ground,
It puts me in the mood,
Up, down, touch the ground,
In the mood – for food!
I am stout, round, and I have found,
Speaking poundage-wise,
That I improve my appetite
When I exercise!"

It goes without saying that, for Pooh, one of the best parts of doing his

Stoutness Exercises was thinking about the Little Something he would have as a treat afterwards!

"Just a few more ups and downs," said Pooh to himself as he reached down to his toes.

But Pooh must have eaten too much honey for breakfast that morning, because all of a sudden he felt something go *pop*! Then he heard an awful *r-i-i-p*-ping

sound. When he turned round to look, he saw that, just as he had feared, one of his seams had burst.

"Oh, fluff and stuff," he said. "I'd better pull myself together!"

Reaching round with his chubby arms, Pooh just managed to grab the loose threads. He pulled hard, and *zip*, his seam was closed again. He tied a good tight knot in the thread.

"There, that's better," he said, with a sigh of relief.

Pooh was just admiring himself in the mirror when he heard another sound. "I know what *that* is," he said with a grin. "That's my rumbly tummy, telling me it's time for Something Sweet!"

And so, humming cheerfully, Pooh went off to gather his honey pots.

Pooh skipped to his cupboard. He sang as he skipped:

"I am short, fat,
Proud of that,
And say with all my might...
With a healthy, happy appetite,
I'm a healthy, happy Pooh!"

But when he checked his honey pots, Pooh found that he hadn't much honey left. He'd eaten most of it for breakfast!

"Oh, bother," he said, trying to get to the very bottom of his favourite honey pot. "Only the sticky part left!"

Just then something flew into the room. Pooh couldn't see it, of course – his head was still stuck inside the honey pot. But he could hear it. It was making a buzzing noise.

"The only reason for making a buzzing noise," said Pooh to himself, "is because you're a bee. And the only

reason for being a bee is to make honey.
And the only reason for making
honey," he said, taking the honey pot
off his head, "is so I can eat it!"

Pooh followed the bee outside and
watched it disappear into a hole in a
tree – a honey tree!

Pooh Climbs the Honey Tree

Pooh scrambled up the honey tree. "Hum dum dee dum," he hummed as he climbed.

"Hum dum dee dum,
I'm so rumbly in my tumbly!
Time to munch an early lunch,
And hum dee dum dum dum!"

Pooh climbed a little higher, until he reached the hole where the bee had disappeared. "Oh, good, I'm nearly there," he said to himself. "Just a little further..."

He was just crawling to the end of a slender branch, when... *Crack!*

19

Pooh went tumbling down, down,
down, bouncing from branch to branch,
till he landed in a prickly gorse bush.

A bee, watching from high in the tree,
found it very funny. But Pooh wasn't
amused at all.

"Oh, bother," he said, as he brushed the prickles from his fur. "I suppose it all comes of liking honey so  much. Now I shall have to think of another way to get up the honey tree."

So Pooh sat and thought. And the first person he thought of was Christopher Robin.

Christopher Robin Helps Out

Christopher Robin lived in another part of the Forest, where his friends visited him every day. Christopher Robin was always there, ready to help his friends with any problems they might have.

On this particular morning, gloomy old Eeyore the donkey had lost his tail again. Kanga and Owl had come with Eeyore to ask Christopher Robin to put it back.

"Don't worry, Eeyore," said Christopher Robin, giving the donkey a comforting pat on the head. "We'll soon have this mended."

Christopher Robin got a hammer and nail. "This won't hurt a bit," he assured Eeyore.

"I know," said Eeyore. "It never does."

Very gently and carefully, Christopher Robin tap-tapped Eeyore's tail back into place.

"There," he said. "Did I put it in the right spot, Eeyore?"

"No matter," said Eeyore glumly. "Most likely I'll just lose it again."

"Cheer up, Eeyore dear," said Kanga. "Why don't you try swishing it?"

"Yes, yes!" said Baby Roo, popping his head out of his mother's pouch.

Eeyore went on grumbling, but he tried waving his tail back and forth.

"It's working! It's working!" cried Roo happily.

"Why, so it is," said Eeyore, sounding almost pleased. "I know it's not much of a tail, but I am sort of attached to it."

Pooh Has a Plan

"Good morning, everyone," said Winnie the Pooh when he arrived at Christopher Robin's house.

"Good morning, Pooh Bear," his friends replied.

"Are you looking for something special this morning, Pooh?" asked Christopher Robin.

"As a matter of fact, I am," said Pooh. "And I think I've found it. It's your blue balloon, Christopher Robin. I don't suppose you'd let me borrow it?"

"Of course I will," said Christopher Robin. "But what do you want a balloon for?"

Pooh looked round to make sure the others weren't listening. *"Honey!"* he whispered.

"But you don't get honey with a balloon," said Christopher Robin.

"*I* do," said Pooh, taking hold of the balloon. "I'll fly like a bee up to the honey tree!"

"Silly Old Bear," laughed Christopher Robin, catching Pooh. "You can't fool bees that way!"

"I can," insisted Pooh. "Take me to a muddy place, and I'll show you."

So Christopher Robin took Pooh to a very muddy place, and Pooh rolled and rolled in a big puddle till he was covered in mud from his ears to his toes.

"Isn't this a clever disguise?" he asked Christopher Robin.

"Umm... I don't know," said Christopher Robin. "What are you disguised *as*?"

"A little black raincloud, of course," said Pooh. "The bees will think that the blue balloon is part of the sky, and that I'm just a raincloud drifting by."

Christopher Robin wasn't as certain as Pooh that the disguise would work, but he gave him the balloon.

"Now, aim me at the bees, please," said Pooh. He went floating up, up, up into the air, till he was high amongst the branches of the honey tree.

Just to make sure the bees *knew* he was a raincloud, Pooh sang a little song as he drifted up towards the top of the honey tree. It went like this:

"I'm just a little black raincloud,
Hovering under the honey tree.
Only a little black raincloud,
Pay no attention to me!
Everyone knows that a raincloud
Never eats honey, no, not a nip!
I'm just floating around,
Over the ground,
Wondering where I will drip!"

Soon Pooh was right up at the part of the tree where the honey was. As he looked into the hole, he saw some bees coming towards him. They were buzzing around noisily.

"Christopher Robin," called Pooh, "I think these bees suspect something!"

The Bees Are Not Deceived

"Perhaps they think you're after their honey, Pooh," said Christopher Robin.

"Maybe," said Pooh. "You never can tell with bees. I'll just have to keep singing." And he sang his raincloud song again.

But the more Pooh sang, the louder the bees buzzed. And when Pooh stuck a paw inside the tree and brought it out covered with honey, their buzzing began to sound very angry.

"I'm just a little black raincloud," Pooh sang bravely. But he was getting just a bit worried – especially when he noticed that his paw was covered with bees as well as honey!

"I say, Christopher Robin," Pooh called. "You could help me to deceive the bees. Open your umbrella and say, 'Tut, tut, it looks like rain!'"

So Christopher Robin got his umbrella and walked back and forth with it, muttering, "Tut, tut, it looks like rain… it looks like rain…"

But the bees weren't fooled. They swarmed out of the tree, heading straight for Pooh.

Poor Pooh was getting really upset now. "You know, Christopher Robin," he called at last, "I think these are the wrong sort of bees! Perhaps I'd better come down now… oh… OOOHHH!"

Suddenly Pooh *was* coming down – a lot faster than he wanted to! The string had come away from the balloon, and Pooh was trying to hold on to the balloon itself. But the balloon was losing air and zooming towards the ground at a frightening speed.

And all the while, the bees buzzed furiously round Pooh.

"I'll catch you, Pooh," called Christopher Robin. Pooh came plummeting through the branches till he landed safely in Christopher Robin's arms.

But the bees weren't about to give up. Still buzzing threateningly, they came rushing after Pooh and Christopher Robin, determined not to let the honey thief get away.

"Oh, Christopher Robin, help!" wailed Pooh.

Grabbing Pooh in one hand and his umbrella in the other, Christopher Robin raced to the muddy place and leapt right into the big puddle.

And there Christopher Robin and Pooh stayed, safe under the open umbrella. It made a good hiding place, and the bees couldn't get to them.

Pooh Stays for Tea

At last the bees went back to their tree, and Christopher Robin and Pooh came out from under the umbrella.

"We *both* look like rainclouds now, Pooh," said Christopher Robin, for they were both very muddy indeed. "You'd better come home with me, and we'll have a nice warm bath."

So the two friends made their way back to Christopher Robin's house. And when they were clean and dry, Christopher Robin invited Pooh to stay for tea.

"I've got just the thing to make your tummy stop rumbling," said Christopher Robin, opening his cupboard door. There stood a row of great big honey pots, each one filled to the brim.

"Oh, thank you!" said Pooh. And he ate and ate, until his tummy was full and he was covered in lovely, gooey honey.

It had turned out to be a splendid day, after all.

So that is the story of Winnie the Pooh's adventure with the honey tree.

Pooh's love of honey got him into many sticky situations. Once, he ate so much honey that he got stuck in Rabbit's doorway. But that's another story.

Grown-ups think that all these stories are make-believe, and that Christopher Robin's friends are just stuffed toys. But you and I know better, don't we?

Of course we do — as sure as there's a Hundred Acre Wood!